Anonymous

The Story of Robin Hood

Anonymous

The Story of Robin Hood

ISBN/EAN: 9783337371838

Printed in Europe, USA, Canada, Australia, Japan

Cover: Foto ©Andreas Hilbeck / pixelio.de

More available books at **www.hansebooks.com**

The Story of
ROBIN HOOD

Popular Edition

Profusely Illustrated

Chicago
M. A. Donohue & Co.

Robin Hood

ROBIN HOOD lived about seven hundred years ago, in England, when Richard the First was King. At that time a large part of the land was covered with great forests, in which deer, wild boar and other game ran wild; and it was near the borders of one of these, called Sherwood Forest, that Robin Hood was born.

From his earliest years he had a great love for all the manly out-door sports and games, and he became very expert at them; above all, in the use of the bow and arrow. He grew so skillful in this that there was no archer in all the country round who could compare with him, and he always carried off the prizes at the shooting matches. Besides this, he had bright wits, and a merry heart; loved a song and a jest; and was liked by nearly everybody who knew him.

But something took place which drove him into a way of life that, otherwise, he might not have chosen for himself. In those days all the game in the forest belonged to the King; it was against the law to shoot it. The King had men in the forest, called foresters, to catch those who did so and have them punished. One day, as Robin Hood was passing through the forest, he met with a party of these foresters. One of them was a man who had a great name as an archer and was

ROBIN HOOD

Robin Hood became a Great Marksman.

jealous of Robin Hood's growing fame. He began to taunt Robin, and at last dared him to show his skill by shooting a deer which came in sight at a great distance. Robin Hood's temper was up; and without thinking, he put an arrow in his bow and let it fly at the deer, which it struck and killed. The forester only became more angry at this feat, which was one he could not do himself, so he said he would take Robin and have him hung for killing the King's deer. Robin started to fly, but the foresters pursued him so closely that he saw no chance of escaping, so he turned and again drawing his bow, sent an arrow into the heart of the man who had begun the quarrel. He dropped dead, while his comrades stood still, not knowing but that they might be served as badly, so Robin

Hood escaped. But as there would now be no mercy shown to him if any of the King's men laid hands upon him, he became an outlaw, that is, he lived in the forest, and got his food by shooting the deer and other game, trying of course not to come in the way of the foresters. Now there were many other young men who, from one cause and another had taken to this kind of life, and Robin Hood soon gathered them into a band of which he was made captain, and which became so strong that in the end they were more of a terror to the foresters than the foresters to them. They wore a uniform of Lincoln green, with scarlet caps; and besides his bow and arrows, each man had a short sword; while the captain carried a bugle-horn with which to call his men when he needed them.

Robin Hood's struggle with
Little John.

They led a pleasant life in the green-wood, but it was an entirely unlawful one, for besides shooting the game, they used to rob rich people who passed through the forest. But Robin Hood, though a robber, was in many ways so good that he was thought well of by most people; for he would not take from those who were poor—instead, he often gave them help. He would not let his men hurt or rob a woman, and when the weak were wronged he took their part.

He gave a proof of this one day when he stopped a knight named Sir Richard of the Lea, who was passing with two followers, through the forest. Robin saw that the knight wore a very sad face, and he asked why this was so. The knight replied that he had met with losses, and had been forced to mortgage his lands to the Abbot of St. Mary's of York, who, if the money were not paid next day, would seize all he had. Robin Hood was touched by the sadness of the knight, and agreed to lend him the sum needed to redeem his lands. The knight departed in great joy, and this kind deed was told far and wide, greatly to the credit of Robin Hood.

Robin Hood's dearest friend, and the next in command to himself, was called Little John. The way in which they came together was this. Robin liked to roam the forest by himself in search of adventures; and one day, as he was passing thus along a forest path, he came to a brook over which a narrow plank was laid. Here, in the center of the plank, he met Little John; it became a question as to which should go back. "Let me pass," said the stranger, "or it will be the worse for thee."

Robin laughed at the idea of any one trying to scare him by threats, and told the stranger to go back or he would put an arrow through him.

"Then," said the other, "thou art a coward, for none other would offer to use a bow and arrows against a man armed only with a quarter staff."

Now Robin Hood was anything but a coward, and could not bear to do that which would give anybody a right to call him one; so he stepped aside and cut for himself a staff of oak.

"Now," said he, "we are equal, we will fight it out, and whichever knocks the other into the water shall be victor."

The stranger was seven feet tall, and though Robin Hood was expert in the use of the staff, he found him more than a match. After they had thumped each other well for a while, the stranger at last hit Robin a blow which sent him into the brook. He waded to the bank while the stranger stood and laughed at him. Then Robin Hood sounded his horn, and his men came running from all sides. When he told them how he had been served they wished to give the stranger a taste of the water too, but Robin, who was very much pleased with his strength and skill, stopped them, and asked the stranger if he would not be one of his merry-men.

"Most willingly," cried he, "and though my name is John Little, I hope you will find that I can do great things!"

The merry-men laughed when they heard the big stranger's name; and one of them said that it should be changed from John Little to Little John, which was done, and he was ever after called that way.

Another time, as Robin Hood was walking through the greenwood, he found a fat friar sitting near a brook, and thought he would have some sport with him, so he said:

"Carry me over the brook, fat friar, or I will beat thee till thou art sore."

The friar, without a word, tucked up his gown and carried him over, but as Robin started off, he cried:—"Stop, my fine fellow, and carry me back or it will cause thee sorrow." Robin took the friar on his back, and carried him over, and set him down, saying:—"Now, take me over once more, fat friar. As thou art twice my weight, it is right I should have two rides to thy one."

The friar again took him on his back, but in the middle of the stream, he threw him in the water, saying: "Now, my pretty youth, let us see if thou canst swim."

Then he went laughing on his way. But Robin was angry, and ran after him, and attacked him with his staff. The friar defended himself, and they fought for a long time without either getting the best of it. Finally, when both were tired out, Robin Hood told the friar who he was, and asked him if he would not like to join his band and be their chaplain. The friar was a jolly fellow, and was quite willing to take Robin's offer. So he became one of the merry-men, and was almost as

The Friar dropped Robin into the middle of the stream.

famous as Robin Hood himself, being known as Friar Tuck.

Robin, before he became an outlaw, had been in love with a young maiden named Marian, but he had not seen her since. Her love for him did not die out, however; and finally her longing to see him became so great that she put on boy's clothes, and went to seek him in the forest. She met him at last; but he did not know her in her strange dress, and she would not, at first, tell him who she was, but drew her sword and dared him to fight. He, of course, soon over-came her; so she took off her cap, and let her beautiful hair fall over her shoul-ders, and then Robin Hood knew her. He still loved her as much as ever, and they were soon married by Friar Tuck, the merry-men celebrating their wedding with great festivity.

ROBIN HOOD

Maid Marian longs to see Robin Hood
again, so putting on boys' clothes,
finds him in the forest.

It was the way of the outlaws when they caught travelers who seemed likely to have much gold or silver about them to take them to dine with Robin Hood. After they had been feasted he would see how much they had, and would make them pay for their entertainment according to their means. One day they brought before him a rich Abbot, the same who had been so harsh with Sir Richard of the Lea. Robin Hood resolved that besides taking his gold, he would put him to shame, so after they had stripped him of all his money, they tied him upon a mule's back, with his face to the tail, and in that ridiculous posture sent him out of the forest, amidst hooting and laughter.

One day, as he was on his way to the town of Nottingham, Robin Hood fell in with a traveling tinker and asked

Friar Tuck marries Robin Hood and Maid Marian.

him for the news. "Surely," said he, "wandering about as thou dost, thou must hear a great deal."

"Ay," said the tinker, "I do, and the latest I have heard is the best."

"What may that be?" asked Robin.

"It is," replied the other, "that at last there is to be an effort made to catch that thief, Robin Hood. He has done mischief enough in this forest. I have a warrant, myself, from the Sheriff of Nottingham to catch him; and it would be worth a hundred pounds to me if I could find him."

Robin laughed to himself at this, but went on talking to the tinker until they came to Nottingham. Here he invited the tinker to go with him to an inn, where he treated him so liberally to ale that he became drunk, and, finally, fell asleep. When he awoke, Robin Hood had gone, and the Sheriff's warrant was missing, too. The tinker called the landlord, and told him of his loss.

"Why," said the landlord, laughing, "thou hast been cheated; that was Robin Hood himself."

The tinker at once started to hunt for Robin again; and was lucky enough to meet him in the forest the next day. He attacked him immediately with a thick club that he carried, while Robin defended himself as best he could with his oaken staff, which was the only weapon he had with him. They fought long, on nearly even terms, until at last Robin's staff broke beneath the stout blows of the tinker, who then called upon him to yield or he would crack his skull.

Robin blew his horn for help, and Little John and another came to his aid.

They seized the tinker and were going to hang him to a tree, but he was such a fine, stout fellow that Robin Hood thought he would like to add him to his band. So 'he proposed that he should join, saying that he would give him the hundred pounds reward which he had lost. This was too good an offer to be refused, so the tinker agreed, and Robin said that as he was a man of *metal* by trade, he hoped he would prove a man of *mettle* by nature.

But it happened, at last, that King Richard had occasion to journey into that part of the country where Sherwood forest lay; and there he heard so much of the doings of Robin Hood, and of the way in which he evaded capture, that he made up his mind that something must be done to put an end to such defiance of authority. But he was advised that it would be useless to try to come at Robin Hood with a force of troops, as he knew the forest so well, and how to hide in it, that he had no trouble in escaping from pursuit when the greater strength of his foes made him choose not to fight.

So the King concluded to go into the forest alone, wearing plain black armor, and without anything to show that he was King; hoping in this way to meet Robin Hood, and learn for himself what kind of man he might be.

He had not ridden many miles before he was called upon to halt by Robin Hood himself, who took him for some obscure knight. The King had been a Crusader, and wore the red cross which was borne by those who had gone to the Holy Land to fight; and as Robin Hood had a great respect for all

The King is ordered to halt by Robin Hood.

such, he addressed the supposed knight in a friendly way, and invited him to come and dine with him.

The King consented, and Robin Hood led him to where the merry-men held their feasts, and they all sat down to a banquet of the best the forest afforded. The guest proved a jolly companion, and did his share in the way of joke and song.

Being curious to know if Robin Hood and his men were as wonderful shots as report made them out to be, the King, after the meal, turned the talk on to the subject of archery, and Robin Hood was soon led into giving an exhibition of the skill of himself and his band. Two rods were set up at a distance which the King, from his knowledge of archery, thought to be too distant by at least fifty paces. But Robin

Hood said that his men must shoot at no nearer mark, and that by their rules he who missed should receive a stout blow as a penalty. When the shooting began, the King could not help expressing his admiration at its accuracy; and the infliction of the penalty in the few cases in which shots were missed made him laugh heartily. Finally he spoke to Robin Hood and said:

"Robin Hood, I have much credit with the King. How would it be if I could get him to forgive thy misdoings? Wouldst thou be one of his men and serve him faithfully?"

This was what Robin wished more than all else in the world. "I would be glad," said he, "to give up the life I lead. I did not like it from the first. Some men praise my deeds; but, for my own part, I hate my way of living.

ROBIN HOOD

King Richard is a brave prince, and if he would but forgive me, he would find me as true and as full of love for him, as any man in his service."

"I am King Richard," said the knight as he stood up with a majestic air; and when he had said this, Robin Hood and all his men fell down on their knees before him.

"Stand up, my brave men," said the King. "You have been thieves, which you should not have been, but you are able to serve me if you will. I will forgive what you have done up to this time, but take care that your acts from henceforth are such that I shall feel no grief for the way I now treat you."

Then Robin and his men arose and gave three cheers for the King.

When the King returned to London, Robin and many of his men went with

When they found that the King was addressing them, Robin
Hood and his men fell on their knees before him.

him, while those who remained were made foresters. Robin rose so high in the King's favor that he became rich, and was made Earl of Huntingdon. He continued to be as kind-hearted as ever, and never refused to help the poor and unfortunate, when it was in his power to aid them.

He lived at court many years; but when he grew to be an old man, a great longing took possession of him to return to the forest and resume the merry life he had led there in his younger days. So he got the King's permission to leave the court, and with his dear friend, Little John, who shared his longing, he sought his old haunts in Sherwood.

He found a few of his old comrades still living there, and spent some time very happily with them. But one day, as he was walking with Little John, he said: "We have shot many deer together, Little John, but to-day I feel as though I could shoot no more."

"Why sayest thou so, dear master," said Little John.

"I know not what ails me," said Robin Hood, "but my fingers seem too feeble to draw the bow. Help me to Kirkley's Priory, Little John, perhaps my cousin, the Prioress, may relieve me by letting a little blood."

So they set out for the Priory, but with all the assistance Little John could give him the walk so fatigued Robin Hood that when they reached there he was very ill.

His cousin received him with great apparent friendship, and Little John left him in her care; but the Prioress, not realizing his weakened condition, bled him too freely.

'I will shoot one more shot, and where the arrow falls, bury me."

When Little John came again he found his master in a dying condition. When he asked Robin Hood if there were nothing he could do for him, he said:

"Bring my bow and arrows, and open yonder window. I will shoot one more shot, and where the arrow falls, there bury me with my bow by my side." So his bow was brought, and Little John supported him while, with all his remaining strength, he shot an arrow out of the window. He fell exhausted, and soon breathed his last.

Then his friend, the heart-broken Little John, and his sorrowing comrades, bore him to the spot marked by the arrow; and there his grave was dug, and he was laid to rest as he had directed, while his numerous friends mourned their great loss.

WHO IS THE THIEF?

WHEN I was a boy, my mother took into the house a small girl, to run of errands and to pick peas. The name of this girl was Sarah. She was not more than twelve years old.

The parents of Sarah were quite poor. They lived not far from our house; and, when we gave Sarah any thing good to eat, she would want to run and take it to her father or mother.

One fine day in June, my mother called up Mary, the girl who used to set the table, and said, "Mary, why have you forgotten to put the bread in the napkins by the side of the plates on the dinner-table?"

"I am sure, ma'am," said Mary, "I put the rolls of bread by every plate not half an hour ago."

"It is strange that they are not there now," said my mother. "Put on some more bread at once."

The next day, it was rainy; but, the day after that, the sky was blue, and the sun bright. Again my mother called up Mary, and said, "What does this mean? There is no bread on the table to-day."

"Well, ma'am, that beats all!" cried Mary. "With my own hands I put the bread at every plate not five minutes ago!"

"Who do you think has taken it?" asked my mother.

"Indeed, ma'am, I can't say for certain," replied Mary; "but I can guess who does it. I think the thief wears a blue calico dress."

"Do you mean to say that Sarah takes the bread?"

"What becomes of all the cake and pie we give her, ma'am? Off it goes to her folks the first chance. Not a bit will that child eat."

"I will not think," said my mother, "that so good a daughter can be a thief."

"Wait and see, ma'am," said Mary.

At the dinner-table, my mother told my father of the loss of the bread, and added, "Mary thinks that Sarah is the thief."

"No, she isn't," said my father. "She hasn't the look of a thief. The girl or boy who does mean things soon shows it in the face. Was the bread stolen that day it rained?"

"No: the two times we have lost it the day has been fair."

"And the window was open both those days, was it not?"

"Yes; but what has that to do with the theft?"

"I will watch to-morrow, and then I will let you know."

So the next day, after the dinner-table was set, my father

stood behind the door, and watched. The day was fair, and the window was open.

By and by, the head of a large dog appeared at the window. He looked round, saw no one, and leaped in. He went to each plate, took the roll of bread and ate it, but did not disturb the table.

My father went to the window and shut it, and there the thief was caught. A noble dog, but thin and hungry. My mother and I came in and saw him.

No owner could be found for the dog; so we kept him, and fed him, and after that he did not steal. We called him Bruno.

As for Sarah, my father gave orders that she should have a nice plate of food every day to take to her father and mother.   UNCLE CHARLES.

THE SPIDER.

I will tell you what my little niece Mary found out about the spider. She learnt it all from books, and told it to me as I now tell it to you.

The spider is very greed'y and very cun'ning. In less than one day, he will eat more than twenty times his weight. If a little boy should get up in the morning, and eat a fat pig, and ten tur'keys; and then, about noon, eat a few more pigs; and, before he went to bed, eat a sheep or two, — he would not do more, ac-cord'ing to his size, than the spider can do.

The spider makes his web so that he may catch flies, moths, and such small things. But, if a bee or a wasp gets caught in his web, he will run and help him to break away; for he does not quite like the ways of bees and wasps.

The spider's eyes are bright: sometimes he has six or eight of them. He can smell, hear, and taste. Once a year, he changes his skin, and has a new set of legs. If one of his limbs gets torn off, he does not mind it much : it will soon grow again.

He has eight legs; and these are joint'ed like a crab's, and have claws at the ends. He has two short fore-arms, with which to hold his prey.

He knows when there is to be a change of weath'er. By watch'ing his hab'its, we can learn to fore-tell a great storm or a great frost. He goes out of his web when rain or a bad storm sets in.

A spider may be tamed. A man in prison once tamed a spider, so that it would come and eat out of his hand.

I will tell you a story in which a spider plays a part. There was once a young prince, who said, that, if he had the power, he would kill all the spiders and all the flies in the world.

One day, after a great fight, this prince had to hide from his foes. He ran into a wood; and there, under a tree, he lay down and fell asleep.

One of his foes passed by, saw him, and, with his drawn sword in his hand, was creeping up to him to kill him, when all at once a fly stung the prince on his lip, and woke him. He sprang to his feet, and the foe ran off.

That night the prince hid himself in a cave in the same wood. In the night, a spider wove her web across the entrance of the cave.

Two men, who were in search of the prince that they might kill him, passed the cave in the morn'ing; and the prince heard what they said.

"Look!" cried one of them. "He must be hid in this cave."

"No," said the other, "that cannot be; for, if he had gone in there, he would have brushed down that spider's web."

And so the men passed on, and did not try to look in the cave.

As soon as they were out of sight, the prince thought how his life had been saved, one day by a fly, and the next day by a spider!

He raised his eyes and his hands to heaven, and made a prayer of thanks to God. He prayed, that, where he could not see why God had given life to this ugly thing and to that, he might learn to trust in God, and to wait for more light.   EMILY CARTER

THERE IS A TIME FOR ALL THINGS.

CHARLES RAY came home from school, and said to his broth'er, "Come, Hen'ry, you have staid in the house long e-nough. There is fine skating on the pond. Get your skates, and let us be off."

"Stop and hear me read this sto'ry in my little mag'a-zine," said Henry.

"I shall do no such thing," said Charles. "We have but an hour for play on the ice. We must go now if we would go at all."

"But this is such a nice sto'ry that I want you to hear it," said Henry.

"I will hear it at the right time, and in the right place," said Charles. "It is play-time now; and I shall not stop to hear you read, though I am as fond of that little magazine as you are."

Henry did not like to give up his wish, and so he be-gan to read a-loud.

Then Charles said, "You are as bad as the man who stopped to scold a boy at the wrong time."

"Tell me a-bout it," said Henry.

"Get your skates and come a-long, and you shall hear a-bout it," said Charles. "It is worth hear'ing."

When the boys were out in the cool air with their skates, Charles told the tale thus: "There was once a boy, who, in try'ing to learn to swim, got be-yond his depth in the wa'ter, and saw that he must drown if he could not get help.

"See'ing a man on a rock near by, he cried out to him to help him. But the man be-gan to talk to him thus: 'My young friend, you did wrong in go'ing into the wa'ter before you knew how to swim. You did wrong in com'ing a-lone to the beach, and go'ing out be-yond your depth. You did wrong ' —

"'O sir! sir!' cried the poor boy, 'please help me *now*, and scold me *af'ter-wards*. I shall drown be-fore you get through your ser'mon.'

"'Do not speak, but hear the voice of wis'dom, my young friend,' said the man. 'Let this teach you nev'er to go be-yond your depth. If you had been a good, wise boy,'—

"Here the boy sank."

"Was the boy drowned?" asked Henry.

"No: he was not drowned. A big wave bore him in, where it was not o'ver his head; and he soon got on his feet, and ran up the beach, and put on his clothes."

"I hope he gave that man a piece of his mind," said Henry. "What a foolish old man he must have been!"

"I do not know what the boy said," said Charles. "I only know that the story ought to teach us that a thing that may be good at one time may not be so good at an-oth'er. The man was to blame in choos'ing such a time as that to preach."

SANDY BAY.

/,,

THE BLUEBIRDS WHO WOULD HAVE THEIR HOUSE CLEANED.

I WANT to tell you a short story about some birds. It is a true story about Mr. and Mrs. Bluebird.

I have a friend who is very fond of all kinds of pets, and, most of all, of birds; and she loves so much to watch them, that she has put two little bird-houses in the trees near her window.

Here, every year, a pair of bluebirds come to make their home for the summer. My friend likes very much to watch them, as they fly round so busily, getting food for their little ones, and, when the warm weather comes, teaching them to fly.

So, very early every spring, my friend has the gardener clean out the houses, and make them quite nice, and ready for the little birds. But this spring, she was busy about other things; and it was so cold and chilly, she scarcely thought of the birds.

But one morning, as she was sitting by her window, she heard a great twittering and fluttering in the old maple-tree. It was Mr. and Mrs. Bluebird, and they were in some trouble.

Mrs. Bluebird would go into the house and look round; and then she would come out and talk away to Mr. Bluebird; and then he would go in, and they would both come out, and chatter and scold.

Then they examined the other house; but it did not suit them any better. They said, just as plainly as birds could, that they would not do their own house-cleaning; and then they flew off.

My friend was very much amused; but she felt sorry too, for the disappointed little birds; so she had the houses all put in good order that very day.

The next morning she was much pleased to see the little birds back again. No doubt they were glad to find their house so nicely cleaned and put in order. They went to work happily and cheerfully to build their nest, and then to go to house-keeping for the summer.

Don't you think they were funny little bluebirds?

CHARLIE'S MAMMA

SOMEBODY'S COMING.

Kris Kringle is coming,
Kris Kringle is coming,
  Kris Kringle is coming to town !
He wears a big pack
On the top of his back,
  And looks like a funny old clown.

Now wait just a minute :
I'll tell what is in it,
  Then won't your eyes sparkle with joy !
There's something with curls
For good little girls,
  And something as nice for each boy.

There are flaxen-haired dollies,
And all sorts of follies,
  To please little folks Christmas Day ;
There are gay horses prancing,
And Dandy Jacks dancing,
  And every thing fitted for play.

From Kris Kringle's chin
Hangs a plenty of tin, —
  Tin trumpets and watches and drums ;

Noah's ark painted red,
A little doll's bed,
  And soldiers with very big guns.

From out of his pockets
He'll take sugar lockets
  And candies, all red, white, and blue ;
And there will be kisses
For nice little misses,
  And sweetmeats in plenty for you.

Oh ! won't there be funning,
And laughing and running,
  When little folks peep in their hose,
And pull out the candy,
And every thing handy, —
  Stuffed full to the end of the toes !

Then hang up your stockings !
Oh ! won't there be knockings
  When Kris Kringle enters the town !
He wears a big pack
On the top of his back,
  And looks like a funny old clown !

AUNT CLARA

16

OLD MAJOR.

EVERY summer, when the warm July days come, we leave our dusty city, and, getting on one of the beautiful steamers that are daily passing, we glide over the lovely Detroit River, through Lake St. Clair and Lake Huron, until we come to the beautiful island of Mackinac.

The island rises like an emerald from the clear waters of the lake; and the pure, life-giving breezes that sweep over it have made it a famous place of resort for those persons in search of health or of pleasure.

We are sure to have a warm welcome from our friends there; and no one of them expresses more gladness at our coming than good old Major.

Major is a large Newfoundland dog; but he and his little mistress Jessie, who is about the same age, are such constant playmates, that he really seems to think himself one of the family.

Jessie and Major always meet us when we land from the steamer; and the first thing that all the children do is to try who shall reach the beach first. There is a hard chase, with much laughing and shouting; but Major gets ahead. because, you know, he has four feet, and the others only two.

When the children tire of the beach, they start for the bluffs, which are high and steep. The one that gets to the foot of the hill first takes hold of Major's tail, and is drawn up in fine style. This is great fun.

In the long twilight, when the children gather on the green to play, they sometimes give Major a ride in the wheelbarrow. Then Jessie will say in a pitying tone, "Poor Maj. is dead!" and tip him out on the grass; and there he will lie as stiff as a stick of wood.

One of the children will raise his head or tail; but it will drop back like lead. Then they all say, "Poor Maj. is dead!"

Pretty soon one of them will say. " I don't believe he is dead: I saw him wink."

Then they all say, "Oh, no! he must be dead;" when up Major springs, and jumps about, and wags his tail, as much as to say, "Didn't I fool you nicely?"

You would laugh to see Major and the little chickens together. When he lies down, they sometimes flock round him, nestle on his back, climb on his head, and peck at his ears.

One day, Fanny called us to the window to look at a smart little chick perched on the middle of his back, and scratching as busily as any chick on the ground.

Now, don't you think Major is a nice old fellow? If you will come up to Mackinac next summer, I will show him to you, and you shall see also the beautiful woods where the children make their play-houses, and a hundred pretty things that I have not time to write about.

DETROIT, MICH.   AUNT HATTIE.

———◦◦}⚬{◦◦———

KINDNESS TO ANIMALS.

IN the sketch on the next page, the artist shows us a scene that is very common in England.

It is a group of children looking at a printed placard. Let us see if we can tell what is printed upon it.

We can read the head-line with ease. It is,—

"THE ANIMALS' FRIEND'S ALMANAC."

The large picture in the middle is plain enough. It is a horse drinking at a fountain. There is a picture of birds at the top. The other pictures we cannot make out.

But we have seen enough to know what the placard means, and why it is put up in such a public place. It is a good word spoken by kind people for the animals, that cannot speak for themselves. A street placard like this is much needed in this country. It ought to be as common as it is in England; for it is sure to attract attention, and answers a very useful purpose.

PUSSY WHITENOSE.

"WHAT a funny name for a cat!" some of you may say, as you read the above title. Well, if you could see the cat herself, you would know why we call her "Pussy Whitenose;" but the picture of her will tell you almost as well.

If you look at it again, you will see that her fore-paws are rather large and queer. They are double paws; that is, on each of them grows an extra toe, with a claw in it, making the foot look something like a mitten. Such paws are sometimes called "mitten-paws."

These large paws look very clumsy; but they are lively enough when after a rat or a mouse; and, when they get hold of one, there is very little chance for it to escape.

When Pussy Whitenose was a kitten, I used to play with

her a great deal, and I taught her to do some funny things. One was this: I would stoop down, put my hand over my shoulder, and snap my fingers. When Pussy heard this, up she would jump, and sit upon my shoulder; and there she would stay while I walked around the cellar.

If I put my hand up on one side, she would whisk around, and rub her head against that hand; and when I changed my hand to the other shoulder, round would come old "Whitey," and push against it, and purr, as if to show how happy she was feeling.

Pussy Whitenose is now an old cat, having lived with us more than eight years; but she has not forgotten her youthful tricks, and I have seen her frolic with her own kittens almost as merrily as if she were a kitten herself.

The other night I went into the cellar to get a hod of coal. Old Pussy was there, having a quiet nap. Just to try her I stooped down, and snapped my fingers, as I used to do. She left her bed in a moment, and jumped up to her old place on my shoulder.

I went about my work, shovelled the coal into the hod, crossed the cellar, went up two flights of stairs to my room, and, putting down the coal-hod, began dancing about, with old Pussy Whitenose clinging to her seat all the while, and purring loudly. I believe she would have staid there all night, if I had not made her jump down, and go back to her bed in the cellar. Theo. Melville.

THE SHOEBLACK'S DOG.

Oh, what a sly dog! Just look at him! What do you suppose he is doing? I think you might guess many times, and not guess right.

I will tell you what that sly dog is doing: he is trying to muddy Mr. Blake's clean shoes. But why should he do that? You shall learn.

Mr. Blake was in the great city of Paris. He walked out on a bridge one day, when this dog, whose name is Nap, came up with muddy paws, and acted as I tell you. Mr. Blake went to a shoeblack near by, and paid him for cleaning his shoes.

The next day Mr. Blake was walking over the same bridge, when Nap again ran up, and soiled his shoes. "I will see what this means," thought Mr. Blake: so he walk on, and stood where he could watch the dog.

Nap ran down by the river's side, and put his paws in the mud, and then came up on the bridge. When he saw a gentleman pass, he would run, and wipe his dirty paws on his shoes; and then the gentleman would go to the shoeblack, and pay him for cleaning them.

"I see how it is!" said Mr. Blake to himself. "That dog belongs to the shoeblack, who has trained him to muddy the shoes of people passing by, so that they may come and give the shoeblack a job."

Then Mr. Blake went up to the man, and said, "Why do you let your dog act in this way?"

"Ah! trade is so bad!" said the man.

"Come, I will buy your dog," said Mr. Blake.

So Mr. Blake bought the dog, and took him to London, where he kept him tied up for some time; but at last he let him go loose. Nap ran away; and, two weeks afterwards, he had found his way back to Paris, to his old master.

How Nap got across the channel I do not know. I only know this is a true story; and I think I never heard of such a sly dog as this same Nap.   TROTTIE'S AUNT.

SEE THIS LITTLE BOY AND HIS SISTER SEATED ON THE BANK, AND WATCHING THE SHEEP.

RECOLLECTIONS OF SUMMER.

ELLEN and Ruth sat on the sofa in the nice warm room where their father kept his books. A fire burnt in the grate; but, out of doors, the wind blew hard, and the snow beat against the windows.

"Don't you remember," said Ruth, "when we used to work in our little garden, with the watering-pot and the rake?"

"Yes," said Ellen; "and don't you remember how I used to get my little basket full of flowers, and bring them in, and fix them in a vase, and then put them on father's table?"

"Yes; and then we would go and rake hay in the fields where the men had been mowing. How sweet the hay used to smell! Oh, I do not like the winter at all!"

"Do not say so, Ruth! Think how much that is sweet the winter brings us. We can slide on the ice; we can drag our little sleds; and we are to have, each of us, a pair of skates soon. It was only the other day I heard you say you were glad to see the snow."

"It is very odd, Ellen; but in winter, when I think of summer, I like the summer best; and in summer, when I think of winter, I like the winter best."

"That shows, my dear little Ruth, that God, who gives us winter and summer, and autumn and spring, knows best what is good for us. Our true way is to be content with every season as it comes, and not to keep finding fault with the weather."

"Yes, that is the true way," said Ruth; "and, though it is so dark and stormy out of doors now, we can sit here before this nice, cheerful fire, and read our good books, and look at pictures of the summer-time, till we almost feel as if we were plucking flowers and raking hay once more."

ANNA LIVINGSTON.

A DIALOGUE FOR GEORGE AND FRANK.

GEORGE.

SOMEBODY's been in the garden,
  Nipping the blossoms fair :
All the green leaves are blackened —
  Who do you think was there ?

FRANK.

Somebody's been in the forest,
  Cracking the chestnut-burrs :
Who is it dropping the chestnuts
  Whenever a light wind stirs ?

A DIALOGUE FOR GEORGE AND FRANK.

GEORGE.

Somebody's been at the windows,
　Marking on every pane:
Who made the delicate drawings
　Of lace-work and moss and grain?

FRANK.

Somebody's all the time working
　Out on the pond so blue,
Bridging it over with crystal, —
　Now can you tell me who?

GEORGE.

While he is building his bridges
　We will patiently wait;
And, when he has them all finished.
　Then we will slide and skate.

FRANK.

And I will hurrah, and you will hurrah —

GEORGE.

And we both will hurrah —
　For Jack Frost!   A. W.

LOVE IS THE BEST FORCE.

ONCE two little boys were on their way to school. They were broth'ers, and their names were John and Frank. John was the old'er of the two, and he liked to rule Frank by sharp words; but Frank did not like to be ruled in that way.

"Come on — quick'er, quick'er. What a slow coach you are!" said John.

"It is not late, and the day is hot," said Frank.

"I tell you I want to get to school in time to clean out my desk," said John. "Come! you *shall* come."

And then John tried to pull Frank a-long by main force; but, the more John pulled, the more Frank made up his mind not to yield.

While the dis-pute went on, they came to a place in the road where a man was try'ing to make a horse pull a great load of stones. The horse had stopped to rest, when the man be-gan to beat him.

This the horse did not like, for he had tried to do his best: so he stood stock still. In vain did the man lay on the lash: the horse would not start. In vain did the man swear at him: the horse did not mind his oaths.

Just then a young man came u_ , and said to the man with the load of stones, "Why do you treat a good, brave horse in that way? He would pull for you till he died, if you would on'ly treat him kind'ly. Stand a-side, and let me show you how to treat a good horse."

So the man stood a-side; and the young man went up, and put his arm round the neck of the horse, and pat'ted him on the back, and said, "Poor old fel'low! It was too bad to lash you so, when you were do'ing your best, and just stopped a mo'ment to take breath."

And so the young man soothed the poor beast, by kind words and soft pats with his hand; and then said to him, "Now, good old horse, see what you can do! Come, sir! we have only a few steps more to the top of the hill. Get up now. Show you will do for love what you would not do for hate."

The horse seemed to know what was said to him; for he start'ed off at a strong, brisk pace, and was soon at the top of the hill.

"There, my good friend," said the young man to the driv'er, "I hope you see now that *love is the best force;* that even beasts will do for you, when you are kind, what they will not do when you are harsh."

John heard all these words, and they set him to think'ing. At last he said to Frank, "It *is* a hot day, Frank; and it is not late. Let us walk through the lane to school."

"No, John," said Frank, "I will take the short cut, and will walk just as fast as you want me to. So, come on."

"Frank," said John, "Love *is* bet'ter than hate, — isn't it?"

"Oh, a thous'and times better!" cried Frank.

As chance would have it, they that day read in school a fa'ble, two thous'and years old, which I will now tell you.

The North Wind and the Sun had a dis-pute as to which could show the more strength. They a-greed that the one that could strip a man first of his cloak should be the ⁻ic'tor.

First the North Wind tried his strength: he blew, and blew, with all his might; but, blow as hard as he could, he could not do much. The man drew his cloak round him more and more tight; he would not let it be torn from him. So at last the North Wind gave up the tug, and called on the Sun to see what *he* could do.

By look'ing at the two pict'ures of the same man, you may see what the North Wind *could* not do, and what the Sun *did* do. The Sun shone out with all his warmth. The man could not well bear the heat: he soon grew to be so warm that he had to take off his cloak; and so the Sun be-came the win'ner in the tri'al.

Love has more strength than hate.   EMILY CARTER

EVENING HYMN.

I HEAR no voice, I feel no touch,
  I see no glory bright;
But yet I know that God is near,
  In darkness as in light.

He watches ever by my side,
  And hears my whispered prayer:
The Father for his little child
  Both night and day doth care.

NOW, CARLO, B IS FOR BARK!

MABEL AND HER GRANDMOTHER.

MABEL and her little sister Jane are orphans. They live with their grandmother, who is very kind to them. In the picture, she is showing the children a likeness of their mother.

With such a pleasant home, and such a loving grandmother, one would think that these two little girls ought to be happy and contented. And Jane, the younger of the two, is as happy as the day is long.

But Mabel, although not a bad child at heart, has an unhappy temper. She is sometimes moody and wayward, and gives her good grandmother much trouble.

I will tell you one of her freaks, and how her grandmother managed her.

One day Mabel had been reproved for some fault, and knew that she had done wrong; but, instead of saying that she was sorry, she brooded over the matter until she persuaded herself that she had been very much injured.

So she said to herself, "I will run away. I will mak.
g ndmother sorry that she has treated me so."

Poor little Mabel! She never stopped to think what
" i nning away" meant, but went softly up stairs to hei
ɔw n room, and began taking out articles of dress from the
bu.eau-drawer.

Just then her grandmother came up stairs, and, seeing
what was going on, knew in a moment what was passing in
Mabel's mind.

"If my little girl is going away," she said very quietly, "I
mu t get her something to pack her clothes in."

Then she brought a little travelling-bag, and Mabel packed her clothes in it.

"I must pay you the fifty cents I promised you the other day," said her grandmother. "Here it is. You may need it."

Mabel began to feel ashamed when she saw the sad look on her grandmother's face. But she was too proud to say so. Pretty soon her bag was packed, and she was all ready.

She could not go without bidding little Jane good-by. Jane was asleep in her crib. Mabel kissed her; and saying, "Good-by, dear Jenny: you may have my fifty cents," she put the money into Jane's little chubby hand.

But now there were tears in Mabel's eyes, and two large drops were rolling down her cheeks.

"Good-by, grandmother," said she.

"Good-by, dear child," said her grandmother. "I hope people will be kind to you *where you are going.*"

Mabel could hold out no longer.

"O grandmother!" she sobbed. "I want to stay with you. I will never, never, be a naughty girl again, if you will only love me once more."

"I have always loved you, my darling Mabel," said her grandmother, giving her a kiss; "and I love you now better than ever. Come now, we will hang up this travelling-bag and you shall be my own dear little girl again." Lila

THE FAWN CHASED BY DOGS.

FAWN is a young deer. I will tell you a true story of one. On a bright summer day last year, a fawn lay nibbling the tender grass on the border of a wood in Oregon. She lay there at ease, as if there were no cause for fear : for the birds sang on the trees ; and under the blue sky floated the clouds, with their white, shining folds turned out to catch the rays of the sun.

All at once the little fawn started to her feet, and pricked up her ears. What did she hear? Ah! It was something more than the sweet twitter of birds : it was the barking of dogs who had scented her track, and were in full pursuit.

Off started the little fawn : and it was well she ran swiftly ; for soon three fierce dogs that had strayed from a farm near by rushed from the woods into the clearing, and by their fierce barking made her heart beat. From the clearing she ran into a grove where the trees grew high and thick ; but the dogs followed close on her path, and she saw they were gaining on her fast.

Now, it happened that Silas Mason was at work squaring timber near his log-hut on the edge of the grove. As his raised axe descended into the timber, he heard the barking of dogs, and, looking up, saw a beautiful young fawn galloping towards him. The next moment the three dogs made their appearance.

Seizing a stout stick, Silas beat them off; and as soon as they were out of sight he turned, and saw the fawn standing by the timber, her dark eyes sparkling, and her neck outstretched as if to be sure that her enemies had gone.

By a strange instinct the fawn seemed to know at once that Silas was her friend, and that but for him she would have been torn in pieces. She let him come up to her, and pat her on the head, and then watched him curiously as he brought water to her in a pail. She took both water and food from his hands, and did not seem at all afraid.

See what kindness will do, even to an untamed animal. For the rest of the day the fawn staid near her protector, and seemed happy in his presence. But the next morning she had disappeared. Perhaps she went to seek her brothers and sisters in the woods.

Some one said to Silas, " Why didn't you shoot her for venison ? " — " What ! " cried Silas, " betray confidence — that of a poor dumb animal — of one who had run to me even for help from her enemies ? No: I would sooner have gone without my dinner for a week than have harmed that little fawn after she had asked me, by her looks, to protect her. No good man will betray confidence."

UNCLE CHARLES.

FEEDING THE SWANS

MORE ABOUT PARROTS.

HERE is a picture of a macaw, which is the largest of all the parrots. It is found in South America, and is known by its bare cheeks, and its long, tapering tail.

Its plumage is very brilliant. The principal species are the red, the blue, the green, and the black.

It is easily tamed, but cannot learn to talk so well as some of the smaller parrots, — such as we have had some stories about in "The Nursery."

We have another good parrot-story, which was sent to us by a little girl in New Jersey, who signs it "Laura Yard, aged thirteen years." We give it in her own words: —

"A friend of mine had a parrot that played a good many funny pranks. Sometimes he would go to the piano, and step on the keys; and, when they sounded, he would say, 'Goodness gracious sakes!' and everybody would laugh.

"My friend had a chair which she did not allow the children to sit in. One day, a lady came to make a call; and, while waiting in the parlor, she was surprised to hear some one say, 'Get right out of that chair!'

"She looked, but could see nobody. She was just sitting down again, when the same voice said, 'Get right out of that chair!'

"Well, she did get 'out,' and took another chair; but she was scarcely seated, before she heard the same voice, 'Get right out of *that* chair!'

"She was about to leave the house, when she saw perched in his cage a parrot, and knew at once where the voice came from.

"Then she laughed, and told the story as a good joke."

A PUZZLING QUESTION.

I WILL tell you a true story of my nephew Willy, who is just old enough to read "The Nursery." He found a likeness of a man, in a book, the other day, and said, "Aunt Susan, is that a likeness of Uncle Charles, the good man who gives us 'The Nursery?'"

"Why, no, Willy!" said I: "that isn't Uncle Charles; that is Shakspeare." "But, Aunt Susan, Shakspeare isn't as great a man as Uncle Charles, is he?"—"Well, Willy, that is a hard question to answer," said I. "I doubt if Shakspeare has as many readers among little boys and girls. I can say that much."   AUNT SUSAN.

BLINDMAN'S BUFF.

COME, boys and girls, and have some fun,
Now that our daily work is done.
Of books to-day we've had enough:
Now for a game of blindman's buff!
So tie a kerchief round George's eyes,
While each to some quiet corner hies,
Or dodges about, as quick as thought,
That he may not be by the blindman caught.
    Hurrah, hurrah! for the merry play.
     "Turn round thrice, and catch whom you may."

Take heed of the fire! Don't strike the chair!
Of the vase on the table pray beware!
See! Frank with a cane tickles blindman's nose,
And Ted in his ear a trumpet blows;
Little Nell has shrunk behind in fear,
And timid Charles loiters far in the rear;
While Eveline joyously jumps about,
And Will on the chair does nothing but shout.
   Hurrah, hurrah! for the merry play.
   "Turn round thrice, and catch whom you may."

J. B.

A TRICK OF MY BLACK PINK.

My Black Pink ran all over the garden; for he was a dog. Now, the garden where he ran was on a small island in the sea: and I will tell you what Pink did one morning.

I was sitting in the sun on the sand; and the sea was all blue and gold; and the baby waves were dancing up and down, as nothing but baby waves can dance. Up above my head, right in the grass, a tiny kitten was hiding; and down on the sand, by my feet, lay Pink. Oh, how black he was! — not a bit of white about him anywhere. He kept his eyes on the grass where kittie was, a few minutes; then up he jumped, and ran right up the bank, and sprang into the grass. All in a minute the dog ran past me again, and in his big mouth *was the little kitten.*

"Pink, Pink! — you naughty dog!" I cried, "come here, this minute." But Pink did not mind me one bit. He just stopped half a second, or about that time, turned his eyes back at me, as if he would like to make them say, "I am only doing my duty, ma'am;" then he gave one solemn wag of his tail, and plunged off into the sea with kittle in his mouth.

I ran down close to the water, and called and begged and scolded; and my Black Pink paid no more attention to me than he did to the rocks on the shore.

Around and around the dog went. Once or twice he dropped the kitten a little way out from his mouth, just to see if it could swim. Then back he came to the shore, laid kittie, all wet and cold, on the sand, shook himself, gave

kittie two or three hints with his paw to get up and shake herself; but kittie did not mind: so Pink rolled her over and over in the sand, until there was such a big bundle of sand that nobody would think there was a kitten inside it.

Then he took up the bundle, and carried it up the bank and laid it in the sun, and stood a long time looking at it.

I picked up the kitten, and was carrying it to the house to rub off the sand and dry the poor thing; and, as I was on the walk, I met John the gardener, and told him what Pink had done.

" Oh! it won't kill the cat," he said. *"Pink gives it a bath every day ; and kittie likes it when she gets dry."*

I am afraid some one will think this a made-up story, if I do not tell you that it is true; that I saw it; and that it happened on a little island in Long-Island Sound, where I have spent many summers, and about which I could tell you stories enough to fill " The Nursery " a whole year.

S. L. P.

———◦◦᠃᠃◦◦———

CHICK-A-DEE.

LITTLE MARY'S SONG.

CHICK-A-DEE! chick-a-dee! chick-a-dee-dee!
The bravest of all little birdies is he.
He comes in the winter; and, cold though it be,
He cheerily warbles his chick-a-dee-dee.

" O Mary! O Mary! sweet Mary!" says he,
" I'm a bright little bird, with a heart full of glee :
Come here and live with me on my willow-tree,
And I'll sing to you, darling!   I'll sing chick-a-dee!"

" O birdie! dear birdie! O good chick-a-dee!
I cannot live with you in your willow-tree :
My own mamma loves me as well as can be;
And what would my dear papa do without me?

" Pretty chick-a-dee-dee, so merry and free,
Come sit, little birdie, on my cherry-tree :
I'll throw you some crumbs from the window, you see,
While you merrily warble your chick-a-dee-dee ! "

WEST NEWTON.   COUSIN LUCY.

THE BIRD–HUNTERS.

"Now for it!" said Albert. "Just stand back, Lucy Keep still, and see me catch those two little birds."

The two little birds did not seem to be much terrified by Albert's approach, though he had his hat all ready to put over them. They continued to play till he got quite near, and then they flew up to a higher part of the tree.

"You ought to get a little fresh salt and put on their tails," said Max, an older boy, who stood near with a stick in his hand.

"There is no such thing as fresh salt," said Lucy: "salt is always salt."

"So it is," said Max; "and you, like the birds, are too wise to be caught."

"If I can't catch a bird, I can catch a butterfly," said Albert. But he tried to catch one, and failed.

Then Max said, "Look here, little ones, my mother says it is wrong to torment birds and butterflies. We ought to be kind to every thing that lives. Come with me, and I will show you where we can pick a plenty of ripe blackberries."

So they went with Max, and picked blackberries. With some large leaves they made a little plate, and put in it berries enough to take home to their mother.   Ida.

GOLD LOCKS.

Gold Locks wears such a cunning cap!
   Delicate are its soft white laces,
Dainty and blue its silken crown :
   Dear little girl, how sweet her face is!

With her Normandy bonnet on,
   Easy it might be to mistake her
For a small-folks' queen from fairy-land,
   Or a quiet, rose-cheeked little Quaker.

Yet she's neither a Quaker nor a queen,
   For all she wears such a funny bonnet;
But her head is the brightest ever seen,
   With grandpa's loving hand upon it.

Clara Doty Bates.

Clarence at the Menagerie

On the first day of May, a big menagerie came to our town; and Clarence went with his papa to see the animals. He enjoyed looking at them all; but most of all he liked the monkeys and the elephants.

He fed monkeys with candy, and laughed to see them hang by their tails while they took it from his hand. They ate all the candy he would give them, and did it in a very funny way.

Clarence's papa said the candy had better be eaten by monkeys than by boys; but I doubt whether Clarence was of that opinion.

Clarence was afraid of the great elephant when his papa first took him near it, and hung back when they came within reach of its trunk.

" Why are you afraid of the elephant, Clarence ? " asked his papa. " I'm afraid he will *trunk* me," said Clarence.

But he soon got over his fear, and was so busy feeding the elephant, that his papa had to coax him away.

On their way home, Clarence's papa told the little boy some stories about elephants. Here is one of them : —

A famous elephant, called Jack, was once travelling with his keeper from Margate to Canterbury in England, when they came to a toll-bar. Jack's keeper offered the right toll, but the toll-bar man would not take it. He wanted to make them pay more than was right. So he kept the gate shut. On this the keeper went through the little foot-gate to the other side of the bar, calling out, "Come on, Jack · " and at once the elephant applied his trunk to the rails of the gate, lifted it from its hinges, and dashed it to the ground. He then went on his way, while the toll-bar man stood petrified to see what a mistake he had made in demanding an unjust toll from an elephant

" Now, Clarence," said his papa, " I suppose you would say that the elephant 'trunked' the toll-gate, and so he did ; but, you see, it was because he did not choose to be imposed upon."

CLARENCE'S PAPA

THE CHILDREN AT GRANDMOTHER'S.

HERE was once a grandmother who had fourteen little grandchildren. Some of them were cousins to one another; and some were brothers and sisters. This grandmother lived in an old, old cottage not far from the sea-beach. The cottage had a long sloping roof; and there was an elm-tree in front of it.

One fair day in June, the boys went down to the sea-beach to bathe, and the girls went out on the lawn to play. Some of them thought they would play " hunt the slipper."

But little Emma Darton, who was a cousin to the rest, said, " I promised my mother I would not sit down on the grass: so, if you play ' hunt the slipper,' I must not play with you; for in that game you have to sit."

Then her Cousin Julia replied, " Nonsense, Emma! It is a bright warm day. Don't you see the grass is quite dry? Come, you must not act and talk like an old woman of sixty. Come and join in our game."

But Emma said, " When I make a promise, I always try to keep it. If to do that is to be like an old woman of sixty, then I am glad I am like one."

" You are the oldest-talking little witch I ever knew for a five-year-old," cried Julia. " If you don't look out, you'll not live half your days."

" I think Emma is right," said Marian, another cousin. " So, if you insist on sitting on the grass, Emma and I will go and sit by ourselves on the trunk of the old fallen tree."

But Julia insisted on having her game of " hunt the slipper;" and Emma and Marian went and sat down on the fallen trunk, and looked on while the rest played.

The next day five of grandmother's little visitors did not seem to be well. Some were coughing, and some were sneezing, and some were complaining of pains in their limbs.

" Why, what is the matter with you, children ? " said the old lady. " If I did not know you were sensible little girls, I should say you had been sitting on the damp grass, — all of you but Emma and Marian."

The cousins looked at one another; but no one spoke aloud. Then Marian whispered to Emma, " Are you not glad you kept your promise to your mother ? "

Emma looked up and smiled, but did not say a word.

DORA BURNSIDE.

THE FLYING WOOD-SAWYER.

ONE day last winter I was cutting maple-logs in the woods with a cross-cut saw. It was about five feet long, and had a handle at each end, so as to be used by two persons together. My brother generally helped me; but, for some reason, he was not with me then, and I was at work all by myself in a rather lonesome place.

I had finished eating my dinner, set my pail under a clump of trees, and commenced my afternoon job; but, as the log was large and hard, I often had to stop and rest a minute. While I was standing still, with my hands upon one handle of the saw, all at once a bird came flying down towards me; and, after resting upon the ground behind the log a few moments, what do you suppose he did ?

Whether he knew I was tired, and thought it was too hard for me to cut the wood all alone, I cannot say ; but suddenly he gave a little spring, and seated himself right on the other

handle of my saw, as you see in the picture, grasping it with all the hands he had, and looking as though he had come on purpose to help me saw that log through.

For my part, I rather think he did help me; for, while he kept his hold upon the other end of the saw, I *rested* faster than I ever did before. I stood as motionless as a statue; for I feared that any movement would scare the bird away.

How soon I should have got through my sawing with his help, I cannot tell. But suddenly he seemed to think of something more important; and away he went, like a streak of sunshine, off into the woods beyond me.

I have never seen my sawyer-bird since then. I call him my "sawyer-bird" because I don't know how else to name him. He was a strange bird to me: but he seemed like a good friend; and I shall always remember him as he looked when trying to help me work that winter's day.

UNCLE WILLIAM.

THE OLD BLIND MAN AND HIS GRAND-DAUGHTER.

SILVER-WHITE his locks are straying
As upon the bench he sits,
While his little grandchild, playing,
Round about him sings and flits.

Calmly there, and unrepining,
Waits he — he is old and blind;
But the sun is brightly shining,
And the soft spring airs are kind.

" Ah ! if he could once, once only,
    See the splendor of the vale !
He, so old and weak and lonely,
    See the trees wave in the gale ! "

Then his little daughter, pressing
    Up against the old man's knee,
With her childish, soft caressing,
    Filled his heart with boyish glee.

Through her eyes once more beholding
    All the glories of the spring,
Now his youth once more unfolding,
    Hope and joy and beauty bring.

FROM THE GER.

PAPA'S STORY.

" Now, papa, for another army story," said little Eddie
as he climbed into papa's lap, and prepared himself to listen.
    Papa closed his eyes, stroked his whiskers ; and Eddie
knew the story was coming.   This is it, —

One day, when we were camping in Virginia, some of us got leave to go
into the woods for chestnuts, which grew there in great abundance.   We
were busy picking up the nuts, when we heard a scrambling in the bushes.
We thought it was a dog.

" *Was* it a dog ? " asks **Eddie.**
" No, it was not a dog."
" Was it a cat ? "
" No, it was not a cat."
" O papa ! *was* it a *bear ?* "

" No, it was not a bear."

" Do tell me what it was ! "

" Well, let me go on with my story, and you shall hear.

It was a fox. How he did run when he saw us! We ran after him. and chased him into a pile of rails, in one corner of the camp.

You see, the soldiers had torn down all the fences, and piled them up for fire-wood. The fox ran right in among the rails; aud, the more he tried to get out, the more he couldn't.

"A fox, a fox!" we shouted; hearing which, all the men, like so many boys, rushed up, and made themselves into a circle around the wood-pile, so that poor foxy was completely hemmed in.

Then a few of us went to work, and removed the rails one by one, until at last he was clear, and we could all see him. With a bound, he tried to get away; but the men kept their legs very close together, and he was a prisoner. We got one of the tent-ropes and tried to tie him.

Such a time as we had! One man got bitten; but after a while foxy was caught. Then what did the cunning little thing do but make believe he was dead! Foxes are very cunning: they can play dead at any time.

He lay on the ground quite still, while he was tied, and the rope was made fast to a tree. When we all stepped back, he tried again to get away. The rope held him fast; but he bit so nearly through it, that we feared we should lose him, after all.

So off rushed one of the boys, and borrowed a chain from one of the wagons at headquarters. With this Master Fox was made quite secure.

We tried to tame him; for, being away from all little children, we were glad of any thing to pet. But it was of no use; for, even when foxes are taken very young, they cannot be tamed. They do not attach themselves to men, as dogs and some other animals do. He would not play with us at all; but we enjoyed watching him, as we had not many amusements.

One day we had to go off on a march, and left our little fox tied to a tree. When we came back, he was gone. We never knew how he got away; but we were not very sorry, for he was not happy with us. It was much better for him to be in the woods with his own friends. If he was smart enough to stay there, he may be living now; but he must be a pretty old fox by this time.

Here papa stopped; and his little boy drew a long breath, as though very glad that the little fox got into the woods again.   MARY MYRTLE.

THE POWER OF GOODNESS.

A TRUE STORY.

ONCE there was a good man whose name was John Kant. He lived at Cracow, in Poland, where he taught and preached. It was his rule always to suffer wrong rather than to do wrong to others.

When he got to be quite old, he was seized with a wish to see once more the home of his childhood, which was many miles distant from where he now lived.

So he got ready; and, having prayed to God, set out on his way. Dressed in a black robe, with long gray hair and beard, he rode slowly along.

The woods through which he had to pass were thick and dark; but there was light in his soul, for good thoughts of God and God's works kept him company, and made the time seem short.

One night, as he was thus riding along, he was all at once surrounded by men,—some on horseback, and some on foot. Knives and swords flashed in the light of the moon; and John Kant saw that he was at the mercy of a band of robbers.

He got down from his horse, and said to the gang, that he would give up to them all he had about him. He then gave them a purse filled with silver coins, a gold chain from his neck, a ring from his finger, and from his pocket a book of prayer, with silver clasps.

"Have you given us all?" cried the robber chief, in a stern voice: "have you no more money?"

The old man, in his confusion, said he had given them all the money he had; and, when he said this, they let him go.

Glad to get off so well, he went quickly on, and was soon out of sight. But all at once the thought came to him that he had some gold pieces stitched into the hem of his robe. These he had quite forgotten when the robbers had asked him if he had any more money.

" This is lucky," thought John Kant; for he saw that the money would bear him home to his friends, and that he would not have to beg his way, or suffer for want of food and shelter.

But John's conscience was a tender one, and he stopped to listen to its voice. It seemed to cry to him in earnest tones, " Tell not a lie! Tell not a lie!" These words would not let him rest.

Some men would say that such a promise, made to thieves, need not be kept; and few men would have been troubled after such an escape. But John did not stop to reason.

He went back to the place where the robbers stood, and, walking up to them, said meekly, " I have told you what is not true. I did not mean to do so, but fear confused me; so pardon me."

With these words he held forth the pieces of gold; but, to his surprise, not one of the robbers would take them. A strange feeling was at work in their hearts.

These men, bad as they were, could not laugh at the pious old man. " Thou shalt not steal," said a voice within them. All were deeply moved.

Then, as if touched by a common feeling, one of the robbers brought and gave back the old man's purse; another, his gold chain; another, his ring; another, his book of prayer; and still another led up his horse, and helped the old man to remount.

Then ...l the robbers, as if quite ashamed of having thought of harming so good a man, went up and asked his blessing. John Kant gave it with devout feeling, and then rode on his way, thanking God for so strange an escape, and wondering at the mixture of good and evil in the human heart.

MARY F. LEE.

THE HEAVENLY FATHER.

CAN you count the stars that brightly
Twinkle in the midnight sky ?
Can you count the clouds, so lightly
O'er the meadows floating by ?
God the Lord doth mark their number
With his eyes, that never slumber :
    He hath made them every one.

Can you count the insects playing
In the summer sun's bright beam ?
Can you count the fishes straying,
Darting through the silver stream ?
Unto each, by God in heaven,
Life and food and strength are given :
    He doth watch them every one.

Do you know how many children
Rise each morning, blithe and gay ?
Can you count the little voices,
Singing sweetly, day by day ?
God hears all the little voices,
In their infant songs rejoices :
    He doth love them every one.

FROM THE GERMAN.

A MORNING RIDE.

MAUD is spending her vacation among the woods and mountains of Maine, where she went with her father and mother about two weeks ago.

One very pleasant morning papa said, "I think we had better take a ride this morning." So Maud was called in to get ready; and Hannah, the good white horse, was harnessed into the buggy.

The buggy had but one seat: so mamma found a nice box, and folded her shawl and put on it; and that made a good place for the little girl, between her father and mother; and they all started on their ride.

They went along a shady road near the river, and soon they saw some geese. Several of them were swimming in the water, and one or two were on the bank. One of these had a sort of frame around its neck, and was standing on one leg.

Maud said, "Why, see that poor goose! It has only one leg; and they have put that frame on so it can walk better." But a few minutes after she looked again, and the goose was standing very comfortably on both feet. So it really had two, but had been curling up one of them quite out of sight.

After riding some time, they came to a ferry, — a place for cross-  ing the Androscoggin River; and papa drove through a pleasant field down to the bank of the river. Here they saw a man cutting grass, and asked him about the ferry-boat. He came up and took a horn that hung on a post, and blew a blast, which the ferry-boy on the other side of the river heard.

When the boy heard it, he began to unfasten his boat, and pull it over; and Maud and her father and mother waited, sitting in the buggy, until the boy brought his boat close to the shore, so that they could drive on to it easily.

Then papa said, "Are you all ready?" and the boy an- swered, "Yes, sir;" and Hannah walked on the boat and stood perfectly still, while the boy kept pulling a strong rope, until he drew the boat, with the horse and buggy and people, safely over to the other side. Then they drove up the bank of the river, and came to a gate, which a little girl opened.

Next they came to a very pleas- ant wood, — so pleasant that papa stopped Hannah in the shade, and said she might rest a little; and mamma and Maud got out of the buggy, and picked the young boxberry-leaves, and the red berries, and pulled long vines of evergreen, and gathered moss.

When papa thought it was time to go, he said, "All aboard!" and they got in, and he drove on. They had not gone far when Maud asked if she might drive. So papa handed her the reins; and Hannah seemed to go on just as well as ever.

After Maud had been driving a little while, her father said he thought she had better give the reins to him. This she did, and they went to the village, stopped at the post-office and then drove swiftly home in season for dinner.   n.

OLD TRIM.

HERE'S brave old Trim: I once with him
　　Was walking near the docks;
We heard a cry, both Trim and I, —
　　The cry that always shocks.

" Help! boat, ahoy! See, there's a boy:
   Make haste, he's going down."
" There! watch him, Trim! in after him!
   We must not let him drown."

Through foam and splash Trim's quick eyes flash
   He strikes out to the place;
And round and round, with eager bound,
   He watches for a trace.

A little hand comes paddling up,
   A face so wild and wan :
" Ah, Trim, he's there! Make haste, take care;
   And save him if you can!"

Oh! brave and bold, he seizes hold;
   His teeth are firmly set:
Now bear him near; there is no fear:
   The boy is breathing yet.

" Bravo, good Trim!" They welcome him,
   And clasp him round for joy;
Then homeward bear, with tender care,
   The pale, half-conscious boy.

O faithful Trim! "Would I sell him?"
   Inquired a curious elf:
" What, sell," I cried, "a friend so tried!
   I'd rather sell myself."   GEO. BENNETT.

CAKES AND PIES.

In the dough !   In the dough!
This is the way we make it go :
Roll it, roll it, smooth and thin ;
Pound it with the rolling-pin ;
Cut with thimbles, and it makes
Just the nicest dolly cakes.

Dolly, now, must have a pie :
We will make it, you and I.
Here's a cunning little tin !
Roll and roll the pie-crust thin ;
Spread it smoothly now within ;
Lay some bits of apple in.
Cover nicely ; let it bake :
That's the way our pies we make.

Dolly may not eat it all ;
Then, if playmates chance to call,
We will give them a surprise
With our little cakes and pies.
All we make is good to eat;
For our hands are clean and sweet ;
And we have such handy ways,
Our dear mother often says,
That she thinks, by all the looks,
We shall soon be famous cooks.   EMEROY HAYWARD

THE TIDE COMING IN.

Julia and Rose were on a visit to their uncle, who lived
near the seaside. They came from Ohio, and did not know
about the ebb and flow of the tide of the ocean. They ran
down on the sandy beach, and seated themselves on a rock.

Their cousin Rodney was not far off, engaged in fishing
for perch. All at once there was a loud cry from Julia, the

elder of the two sisters. The water had crept up all round the rock on which they sat, thus forming an island of it; and they did not know what to make of it.

"The water has changed its place," shouted Rose.

Rodney was alarmed, and began to blame himself for neglecting, in his eagerness to catch a few fish, the little girls under his charge.

He took off his shoes and stockings, rolled up his pantaloons, and ran into the water over the sandy bottom to the rock. Taking Rose in his arms, he told Julia to follow.

"But I shall wet my nice boots," said Julia.

"Then, wait on the rock," said Rodney, "while I carry Rose, and set her down on dry land. I will then come for you, and carry you pickback to the shore."

"No, Cousin Rodney," said Julia: "I think I will not ride pickback. I should be too heavy a load. I must not mind wetting my boots and stockings."

"Then, place your hand on my shoulder, and come along," said Rodney. "The tide is gaining on us very fast."

"I don't know what you mean by the tide," said Julia.

"Why, cousin," said Rodney, "you must know that the tides are the rise and fall of the waters of the ocean. It will be high tide an hour from now; then the water will cover all these rocks you see around us. After that, the water will sink and go back till we can see the rocks again, and walk a long way on the sand; then it will be low tide. But we must not stay here talking: the water will soon be too deep for us."

So Rodney took Rose in his arms, and Julia placed her left hand on his right shoulder; and in this way they went through the water to the dry part of the beach.

"We must look out for this sly tide the next time," said little Rose as she ran to tell papa of their adventure.

UNCLE CHA

Music by T. CRAMPTON.

VOICE AND PIANO.

p Moderato.

1. When the moon is shin-ing Brightly in the sky, Lit - tle birds lie
2. Lit - tle lambs that briskly Run, and skip and play, All a - mong the

snug - ly In their nests on high. Not a wing they flut - ter,
mead-ows, Thro' the sum-mer day. Rest within the sheep-fold,

cres.

Not a chirp is heard, Oh! to sleep so soundly, As a lit - tle
Each be - side its dam,— Oh! to be as hap - py As a lit - tle

f

bird, ... Oh! to sleep so soundly, As a lit - tle bird.
lamb; .... Oh! to be as hap - py! As a lit - tle lamb.

GOOD-NIGHT AND GOOD-MORNING.

A FAIR little girl sat under a tree,
Sewing as long as her eyes could see;
Then smoothed her work, and folded it right,
And said, "Dear work, good-night! good-night!"

Such a number of rooks came over her head,
Crying "Caw! caw!" on their way to bed,
She said, as she watched their curious flight,
"Little black things, good-night! good-night!"

The horses neighed, and the oxen lowed;
The sheep's "Bleat! bleat!" came over the road
All seeming to say, with a quiet delight,
"Good little girl, good-night! good-night!"

And what do you think were the last words she said
As mamma led her darling at night up to bed?
"When I'm a big lady, and go to housekeeping,
I sha'n't leave a cobweb for spiders to sleep in."

MRS. H. F. HARRINGTON.

LITTLE ANNA.

 THIS is the cottage where little Anna lived. She ran out, and played all day in the green meadows, and was as happy as a bird.

 A great golden butterfly was resting on a flower. Anna ran to catch it; but away it flew, up into the bright blue sky.

Then she sat down among the lilies, and kissed their red lips, and said, "Pretty, pretty, pretty!" That was all she could say.

 There was a little lamb feeding in the meadow. Anna went up to it, and patted its soft white wool with her hands.

 Then she ran down to the little brook that flowed through the meadow, and there she saw her face in the clear water.

When she was tired, she lay down under a bunch of lilies, and went to sleep. There is where her mother found her, asleep among the flowers.

W. O. C.

If wishes were horses, beggars would ride;
If wishes were watches, I'd wear one by my side.

THE LITTLE BOY'S REBUKE.

THERE was once a very old man who lived in the house of his son. The old man was deaf; his eyes were dim, and his legs weak and thin. When he was at table he could hardly hold his spoon, so much did his hand shake; and at times he would spill his soup on the cloth.

All this vexed his son and the son's wife; and they made the old man sit in a corner behind the stove. There he ate his food from an earth'en-ware dish; and he had not always too much to eat, as you may guess.

Well, one day his trem'bling hands could not hold the dish: it fell on the floor, and broke. At this his son and his son's wife were so vexed that they spoke harsh'ly to the poor old man. His only an'swer was a deep, sad sigh. They then brought him a bowl made of wood, out of which he had to take his food.

Not long after this, his little grand'son, a boy of about four years of age, was seen at work with a chis'el and ham'mer, hol'low-ing out a log of wood.

His parents could not guess what he was trying to do. The little boy said nothing to any one, but kept at work on the log, and looked very grave, as if he had some great work in hand.

"What are you do'ing there?" asked his father. The little boy did not want to tell. Then his mother asked, "What are you do'ing, my son?"

"Oh!" said he, "I am only making a little trough, such as our pigs eat out of."

"But what are you making it for, my son?"

"I am making it," said he, "for you and father to eat out of when I am a man."

The parents looked at each other, and burst into tears.

From that time forth, they treated the old man well. He had the best place at the table, a nice dish, and plenty of food.
UNCLE CHARLES.

SPRING VOICES.

"Caw! caw!" says the crow:
"Spring has come again, I know;
For, as sure as I am born,
There's a farm'er planting corn.
I shall break'fast there, I trow,
Long before his corn can grow."

"Quack! quack!" says the duck:
"Was there ever such good luck?
Spring has cleared this pond of ice;
And the day is warm and nice,
Just as I and Goodman Drake
Thought we'd like a swim to take."

"Croak! croak!" says the frog,
As he leaps out from the bog:
"The earth is warm and fair;
Spring is here, I do declare!
Croak! croak! I love the Spring;
Come, little birds, and sing."

THE OLD YEAR AND THE NEW.

THE north winds blow
O'er drifts of snow:
Out in the cold who goes from here?
"Good-by, Good-by!"
Loud voices cry.
"Good-by!" returns the brave Old Year;
But, looking back, what word leaves he?
"Oh, you must all good children be!"

A knock, a knock!
'Tis twelve o'clock!
This time of night, pray, who comes here?
Oh, now I see!
'Tis he! 'tis he!
All people know the glad New Year:
What has he brought? and what says he?
"Oh, you must all good children be!"

MARIAN DOUGLAS.

A LITTLE GIRL'S PETS.

WERE you ever on a mountain? I have been; and I know a young lady who lived on the top of a mountain all the time that she was a baby and a little girl.

Her name is Fanny; and, when she was a child, she had large dark eyes, and long curls that reached below her shoulders. When she was quite a little girl, she had a big brown dog called Bess.

Fanny and Bess were always together, and were very fond

of each other. Sometimes Fanny was naughty, and her mother sent her to her chamber to stay alone. One day she was sent, and she sat and cried: it was warm weather, and the window was open.

By and by Bess was heard running round and round the house; and presently she darted in at the door, and bounded up stairs to little Fanny's door, who heard her, and let her in.

Then Bess looked up at Fanny with her great sober eyes, as if to say, " What *is* the matter ? " And Fanny sat on the floor beside her, and put her arms around her neck, and told her all about being sent up stairs for being naughty.

While she was speaking, the dog sat quite still and listened; but when she had finished her story, and began to cry, Bess threw back her head, and whined and howled till she could be heard all over the house.

After that, whenever Fanny was sent to her chamber, she used to open the window so that Bess could hear her cry; and the brown dog was sure to come to pity her.

Fanny had a little fox for a pet: his name was *Foxy ;* and very pretty he was, too, with a fresh blue ribbon on his neck every morning. He had a bark that sounded more like a laugh; and, very early in the morning, he would come out in front of the house, and laugh in his queer way, to let them know he was out.

When he was a little fox, he was fed on sponge-cake and milk, and Fanny was careful not to let him taste chicken bones. But by and by he got a taste ; and then people in the village at the foot of the mountain began to miss their chickens.

Foxy used to be up as early as ever; but at breakfast-time he would be missing, and, when he came home later every morning, he had no appetite for breakfast. At last he was caught killing a chicken ; and so one of the men had to shoot Foxy.   L. O.

DOGS AND DOCTORS.

THERE was once a good doc'tor who took a lame dog home and cured him. This doctor soon had a vis'it from the same dog, who brought another dog who had hurt his foot.

And so the good doctor had to cure this sec'ond dog also. You may see a pic'ture of the two dogs at the doctor's door. Was it not odd for a doctor to have a dog for a patient?

Not long ago, one eve'ning, as I sat writing, the door-bell rang. I opened the door, and a man asked, "Is the doctor at home?"

"No," said I; "but he will be back soon."

The man had a dog with him; and this dog came into the en'try and smelt round, and then went off with him.

I sat down again, but had not been seat'ed more than half an hour, when I heard a whin'ing and scratch'ing at the door.

I thought, "Well, here is old Boz." Boz is a dog who lives near by, and comes in at times. So I opened the door. But, in-stead of Boz, the dog who had come with the man a short time be-fore ran in.

He jumped up on me, smelt of my clothes, and then ran all round the room, smell'ing and snuff'ing here and there.

Still he was not sat'is-fied, but kept whi'ning, and look'ing up at me, as much as to say, "You are not the doctor! Where is the doctor?"

At last he went to the door of the doctor's study, and scratched till we let him in.

But, on seeing that the doctor was not there, he scratched

to get out, and then ran off to his mas'ter to tell him, as well as a dog could, that the doctor was not at home.

Was he not a good dog to come a second time to the house to find the doctor? How did he know that his master wanted the doctor?

A. N.

NN and her little sister Mary went out to the pasture one bright summer day, to see the old horse. The horse stood in the shade of the great elm-tree; and, as the two girls came up, he put his head over the fence, as though he was glad to see them.

"Let me feed him," said Mary; and she plucked a bunch of clover to give to the horse.

But, when she held it to his mouth, he reached out for it with his upper lip, and gave a slight snort that startled the little girl. She drew back timidly.

"Don't be afraid," said Ann. "He will not hurt you. Good old horse! See me pat him on the head."

Then little Mary took courage, and let the old horse eat the clover from her hand.

Now I must tell you something about this old horse. Mary's father, who was a doctor, bought him when he was a colt, and named him Hero. For many and many a year he carried the doctor on his rounds, and served the whole family faithfully.

He was older than the oldest of the doctor's children; and was such a gentle, steady, useful creature, that they all became much attached to him.

By and by, Hero grew so old that he was not able to do his usual work. One day a man said to the doctor, "That horse is of no use to you now. Sell him to me. I will give you twelve dollars for him. I want him to work in my treadmill."

Wasn't there an outcry in the house when the folks heard this? The idea of selling old Hero to be worked in a treadmill! That was too bad. But the doctor's answer to the man settled the matter very soon.

"My friend," said he, "there is not money enough in your town to buy this horse for a treadmill."

Soon after this, old Hero got so lame that he was not fit to work at all. Then somebody said, "That horse is good for nothing. I would kill him if I were you."

There was another outburst in the family when the doctor told this. "Papa," said Mary, with her lip quivering, "if you let old Hero be killed, you will be a cruel man."

"That's just what I think," said the doctor. "No, old fellow," said he, patting Hero, "you shall not be killed. You shall have no more work to do. You shall take your ease. You shall have the best stall in the stable, and we will take care of you as long as you live."

So, after that, Hero was one of the family pets. In the summer, his shoes were taken off, and he was put in the richest pasture to roam at will.

He lived upon the fat of the land, and grew so strong and hearty, that, when I last saw him, the old, broken-down horse was frisking about like a young colt.

I wish that all horses could have such a happy old age.

Uncle Sam

LAZY RALPH.

I KNOW a boy, who, when he is sent to do a thing, is apt to play by the way; or else he will stop, and look at a bird or a dog, till it is too late for him to do what he has been told to do.

One day he was sent with a note to a man who lived near a creek; but, when he came to the bridge, Ralph thought he would stop, and look from the bridge at the fish in the creek.

He had some crumbs of bread, and these he threw to the fish; and he thought it was fine fun to watch them, as they tried to get the crumbs.

He staid an hour or more on the bridge, and then went on to give the note to the man; but the man had left the town when Ralph got as far as his house.

Now, this man was a doctor; and the note was to tell him to come and see a girl who was quite ill, and who might die if he could not come quick.

Ralph, by his bad, idle ways, might thus have caused the death of a poor girl; but I am glad to say she got well. And, from that time, Ralph made up his mind that he would change his ways, and, when told to do a thing, do it at once.

SEE THE TWO SWANS SWIMMING ON THE POND.

BILLY HOOD.

T. CRAMPTON.

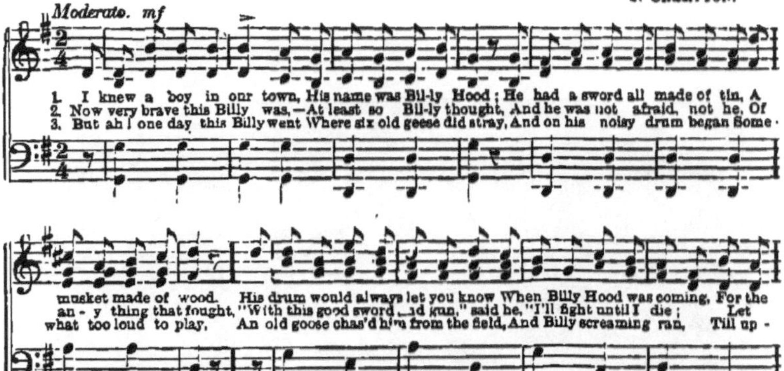

Moderato. mf

1. I knew a boy in our town, His name was Bil-ly Hood ; He had a sword all made of tin, A
2. Now very brave this Billy was,—At least so Bil-ly thought, And he was not afraid, not he, Of
3. But ah! one day this Billy went Where six old geese did stray, And on his noisy drum began Some-

musket made of wood. His drum would always let you know When Billy Hood was coming, For the
an - y thing that fought, "With this good sword and gun," said he, "I'll fight until I die ; Let
what too loud to play, An old goose chas'd him from the field, And Billy screaming ran, Till up-

neighbours al-ways used to say, "I wish he'd stop that drumming; Row de dow, dow,
man or beast come on, who cares? Not Bil - ly Hood; not I !" Row de dow, dow,
- on the kitchen floor he sank, This valiant lit - tle man! Row de dow, dow,

dow! Row, dow, dow! Row de dow de, row de, dow de, row, dow, dow!

THE GLEANERS.

COME to the cornfields! * who will go?
To the golden cornfields! who will go?

* The "cornfields" here referred to are the cornfields of Europe, which in this country
would be called fields of wheat or other grain. The poppy, which is here only seen in gardens
grows there as a common weed in the cornfields.

Where the full-eared corn lies low,
And the scarlet poppies blow, —
      Who will go ?

Underneath these skies of blue, —
Bright and happy skies of blue, —
There is work for all of you, —
Kate and little Harry too,
      Work for you.

The busy gleaners they are here, —
Young and old, they all are here.
Work now like the busy bee, —
Like the busy honey-bee, —
      Help, children dear !   GERDA FAY

A PRESENT FOR MARIA.

Do you see what Thomas, the gardener, is giving to Maria ? It is a pretty little canary-bird in a cage. Thomas has bought it on purpose for her.

He makes her a present because he likes her. She has always been kind to him; and what pleases him still more is, that she has been kind to his little boy, — the boy who is playing with the wagon.

Do you see what that little boy holds with his left hand ? He holds two red apples. Maria has just given him those apples. He is greatly pleased with them. He will not drop them if he can help it; but he must try to move the wagon with his other hand.

The other little boy in the picture is Maria's brother Paul. I am sorry to say that he is not a very good boy. He is not pleased to see a present given to his sister. He wonders why presents are not given to him.

I can tell you the reason, Master Paul. It is because you

think only of yourself. You never try to please anybody else. You must learn to be obliging and friendly to others if you would have them care for you.   ALFRED SELWYN.

HOW ROSE TOOK CARE OF THE CHILDREN,

A FEW years since, there was a little boy named Nelson, who lived in London. He was seven years old; and he had a sister two years younger, and a brother three years younger, than himself. The parents of these children were poor.

One day, when Nelson was coming back from an errand for his mother, a poor little terrier-dog followed him. This dog seemed weak and hungry; his feet and legs were covered with mud, and one of them was lame.

"What is the matter, little dog?" asked Nelson; and, hearing these kind words, the little dog trotted after the boy more boldly, as if he had found a good friend.

On looking closer, Nelson saw that there were lumps on the dog's side, as if he had been beaten with a stick. When the boy reached his home, the dog waited outside on the doorstep.

The children came out to see him; and the dog had such a look of sorrow in his large dark eyes, that it made them cry with pity.

"Do let us keep him, mother, and take care of him," said they; "for he has been badly used."

The mother wished her children to be merciful and kind; so she let the poor dog lie in the wash-house for the night, and gave it some food. The children called the dog Rose; for that was the prettiest name they could think of.

In a few days, Rose grew to be quite strong and well; and he showed his gratitude for kindness in a wonderful manner.

He guarded the house, took care of the hens and chickens, and, what was best of all, went daily with the children to school, and fetched them home.

Now, there was a bad place to cross in the road to the school, and the eldest boy found it hard to take care of his little brother and sister in getting across this place.

Rose seemed to know what ought to be done. He would walk before the children to the edge of the sidewalk, and then, if he saw a carriage coming, he would bark at the children, and run round them, as if they were a flock of sheep he was taking care of.

He would not let one of the children cross until he saw it was safe, and the road was clear, so that they would not be run over; and then he would lead them across, and so frolic along until he came to the school.

Leaving the children at school, Rose would trot home. By and by, the good mother would say, "Rose, it is time to fetch the children;" and then this faithful dog would run to the school, and bring the children home in the same way he had led them before.

As winter came, he would carry their dinner-basket for

them; and sometimes he would even carry an umbrella for them in his mouth. For three years the good dog kept up this care, and then the children were old enough to take care of themselves.

But they did not forget their good dog Rose. This story is a true one, and I think you will see in the picture a true likeness of this good little dog.   Uncle Charles

SHADOW BUFF.

In this game, a large white cloth or sheet is stretched tight against the wall; and the child who plays Buff sits before it in such a way that he cannot see his comrades. The children then disguise themselves as much as possible, and throw their shadows on the sheet. If Buff recognizes one, he calls out the name, and they change places.

K3

BROTHER AND SISTER.

I CALLED at a house the other day; and, as I sat in the parlor, I heard voices from a room near by.

"Wait till I have done with the book, will you? I hate to have girls look'ing over my shoul'der," was said in a boy's voice.

"How rude!" said another voice, which came from a little girl. "I wouldn't be as self'ish as you are for all the world."

"And I wouldn't be a fussy old maid like you for a good many worlds," said the boy.

"I am eight years old," said the girl; "and, if I am an old maid, I shall keep so if the boys grow up as bad as you are."

"Stop that noise, will you, and let me read," said the boy. "It is noth'ing but buzz, buzz, where *you* are."

But I will not tell you all the un-kind words that passed be-tween this boy and his sister. I was grieved and shocked to hear them.

In the next house at which I called, how sweet was the change! As I looked in at the win'dow, I saw a brother and sister sit'ting in the same large chair, and read'ing from the same book.

They had lost their mother, and their father was away at sea. How sad would have been the lot of these chil'dren if they had been rude and cross to each other!

But love made them kind and thought'ful. The broth'er had no rel'ish for a pleas'ure he could not share with his sister; and the sister found her best joy in help'ing her brother to be cheer'ful.

So should it al'ways be be-tween brothers and sisters. Let them shun harsh words. Let them learn the peace and the joy of a lov'ing heart.   ANNA LIVINGSTON.

JACK FROST.

My name and my call'ing, I will not dis-sem'ble ;
JACK FROST is my name, Tom ! Hear that, Tom, and
trem'ble !

LITTLE BOY.

Oh! you are the Frost, then, whose touch is so bit'ter ;
Who made all our win'dow-panes spar'kle and glit'ter !

JACK FROST.

Yes, I am that Frost ; and now, Tom, I am com'ing,
To nip you, and pinch you, your fin'ger-tips numb'ing.

LITTLE BOY.

My fin'gers lie snug in my gay lit'tle mit'tens ;
And the fur of my cap is as warm as a kit'ten's.

JACK FROST.

I will breathe on your ears till they tin'gle, — so, fear me,
And scam'per, Tom, scam'per! — Boo-hoo! Do you hear
me!

LITTLE BOY.

I hear you — I know you — and, if you can match me
In run'ning and sli'ding, come, catch me, Frost! catch me !

JACK FROST.

Stop! stop! — He is gone, all my ter'rors de-fy'ing ;
To scare boys like Tom, I may well give up try'ing.

EMILY CARTER

PAPA'S BOOTS.

SEE Edwin! He is trying on Papa's boots. I think he will find them too large. Edwin is in a hurry to be a man. Be patient, Edwin! Time will fly fast. Be a good boy, and you will be a good man. A happy New Year to you!

IN PEACE PREPARE FOR WAR.

I HOPE there is not to be a war. See! Ann is teaching John to go through the drill. "Forward, march!" cries Ann. And John stands up straight, and marches like a brave soldier. We must not go too near his gun.

THE JUMPING-JACK.

Ann has bought a jumping-jack for her brother John.
She is showing it to him. Ann pulls the string, and the
jumping-jack throws up its arms, as much as to say, "What
do you think of that?" John's eyes open wider and wider.
He thinks it is a most won'der-ful thing.

THE RECRUIT.

CHARLES. Now, Corporal, here is your musket. Attend
to the word of command.

CORPORAL. (*Wags his tail.*)

CHARLES. Shoulder, arms! Hold up your head. Turn
out your toes. That's good.

HENRY (*clapping his hands*). Well done! Well done!

THE FIRST LESSON.

CORPORAL, the dog, takes his first lesson in good manners. Charles teaches him to shake hands, and shows him which is his right paw, and which is his left. Corporal learns so quickly, that Henry, who is looking on, is quite surprised.

LITTLE MOLLY.

There's company coming, there's company coming,
    There's company coming to tea!
So now, little Molly, lay by the big dolly,
    And come and get ready with me.

I'll put on your dress that is braided with blue,
And tie on your shoes that are shining and new,
And curl up your locks like a princess's hair;
And then you must sit yourself down in a chair,
As calm as a clock and as still as a mouse,
And wait till the company come to the house.

And when they appear, oh! be careful, my dear:
I can't allow any loud noise while they're here.
The books on the table be sure not to touch;
And don't ask me questions: you mustn't talk much;
And yet don't be shy, and hide back of my chair,
And only look out with a pout and a stare.

Don't finger your belt like a vain little miss;
And, if one should happen to ask for a kiss,
Don't, shrugging your shoulders, behave like a dunce,
But put up your lips, and go kiss him at once.

That's the suitable way for a maiden of three
To entertain visitors! — chick-a-dee-dee!
So now, little Molly, lay by the big dolly,
    And dress for our company tea!   Marian Douglas

THE PEAR ON THE GROUND.

 A LITTLE boy, as he walked home from
school, saw a ripe pear lying on the
ground in the front yard of a large,
fine house. It was a nice, yel'low
pear. The little boy was hungry.
"How I would like that pear!" thought
he. "I might reach it through the slats of the fence. No
one sees me." Hardly had the thought come to him than
he called to mind these words, THOU GOD SEEST ME.

He at once turned his head away from the pear, and walked
bravely on. But he had not gone far when a little girl came
running after him, and said, "My mother sent me with this
pear to give to you, little boy. She saw you through the
blind as you looked at it, and sends it to you with her love."

BY THE FIRE.

Down in the darkness there twinkles a light:
Fanny is choosing our apples to-night, —
Great ruby-red ones and golden and green,
Ripest and sweetest that ever were seen.

Grandmother sits in her snowy white cap,
Smiling, and smiling, her work on her lap,
Looking so dreamy, she's thinking, I know,
Of happy times vanished, oh, long, long ago!

How the wind whistles! What care we for that?
Windows may rattle, and blinds go rat-tat:
While we are nestled, all cosey and warm,
Close by the fire, we can laugh at the storm.